Over in the Grasslands
Where they really can run
Lived a friendly mother zebra
And her little *calf* one.

"Gallop," said the mother.
"I gallop," said the one.
So they galloped on the plains
Where they really can run.

Over in the grasslands
Where acacia trees grew
Lived a tall mother giraffe
And her little *calves* two.

"Slurp," said the mother.
"We slurp," said the two.
So they slurped up the leaves
Where acacia trees grew.

Over in the grasslands
Running wild, swimming free,
Lived a huge mother elephant
And her little *calves* three.

"Squirt," said the mother.
"We squirt," said the three.
So they squirted with their trunks
Running wild, swimming free.

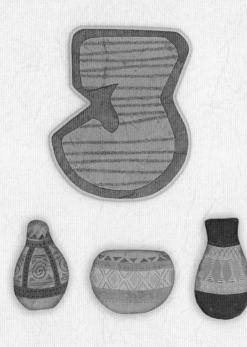

Over in the grasslands
Where they ate more and more
Lived a hungry mother hippo
And her little *calves* four.

"Graze," said the mother.
"We graze," said the four.
So they grazed on the plains
Where they ate more and more.

Over in the grasslands
Knowing how to survive
Lived a proud mother lion
And her little *cubs* five.

"Stalk," said the mother.
"We stalk," said the five.
So they stalked in the grass
Knowing how to survive.

Over in the grasslands
Doing all kinds of tricks
Lived an agile chimpanzee
And her little *babies* six.

"Swing," said the mother.
"We swing," said the six.
So they swung in the trees
Doing all kinds of tricks.

Over in the grasslands
In a tree that points to heaven
Lived a pretty mother hornbill
And her little *chicks* seven.

"Toot," said the mother.
"We toot," said the seven.
So they tooted loud and long
In a tree that points to heaven.

Over in the grasslands
Where they often go out late
Lived a busy mother aardvark
And her little *cubs* eight.

"Dig," said the mother.
"We dig," said the eight.
So they dug up some termites
Where they often go out late.

Over in the grasslands
Where they make a shrill whine
Lived a clever mother meerkat
And her little *pups* nine.

"Watch," said the mother.
"We watch," said the nine.
So they watched and they stood
Where they make a shrill whine

Over in the grasslands
In a rocky-covered den
Lived a cunning father jackal
And his little *pups* ten.

"Yip," said the father.
"We yip," said the ten.
So they yipped and they yapped
Near their rocky-covered den.

Over in the grasslands
Come, let's take a peek!
While their parents all are resting
The kids play "hide and seek."

"Find us," say the children,
"From ten to one."
Then go back and start over
'Cause this rhyme isn't done.

Look for a hidden animal.
You can spy with your eyes,
To find more grassland creatures—
Every page has a surprise!

Find Us!

10 Jackals

9 Meerkats

8 Aardvarks

7 Hornbills

6 Chimpanzees

5 Lions

4 Hippos

3 Elephants

2 Giraffes

1 Zebra

Desert

Rainforest

Grassland

Mediterranean scrub

Fact or Fiction?

In this "Grasslands" variation of the classic children's song "Over in the Meadow," all the African animals behave as they have been portrayed—zebras *gallop*, elephants *squirt* and chimps *swing*. That's a fact! But do they have the number of babies as in this rhyme? No, that is fiction! Elephants usually have one baby at a time, as do mother giraffes and chimps. But in this story elephant mothers are shown with three babies, giraffe mothers are with two, and chimpanzee moms are with five, so that the poem can rhyme!

Baby animals are cared for in very different ways, depending upon the species. Both mother and father jackals take care of their pups, who stay with them until they can establish their own territories. A mother lion will care for her cubs without help from the father, nursing them for about six months and then showing them how to find food on their own. But both hornbill parents help raise their young. While the female sits on her eggs, the male brings her food. Nature has very different ways of ensuring the survival of species.

Life on the African Savanna

Large areas of grass are called by different names on different continents. In North America they are called *prairies*, in Asia and Europe *steppes*, in South America *pampas*, and in Australia *rangelands*. Africa's grassland is called a *savanna* (sometimes spelled *savannah*). It's a sea of grass dotted with shrubs and trees that covers almost half of the continent.

The savanna is home to an abundance and diversity of animals. Although the wet season brings torrential rains, the savanna is warm all year long; and the animals have adapted to dry, windy conditions.

Two of the world's largest animals live on the savanna—the African elephant (largest land mammal) and the ostrich (largest bird). There are more species of hoofed animals living on the savanna than in any other place in the world. They include antelopes, wildebeest, giraffes, zebras, and rhinos. Hoofed animals need to stay constantly on the move as they look for fresh supplies of food and avoid predators like lions and hyenas.

The African savanna has been harmed by humans in a variety of ways over many years, including hunting and overgrazing. Some people and organizations are now taking action to preserve the amazing African savanna biome before it is too late.

Who Are the "Hidden" Animals in the Grasslands?

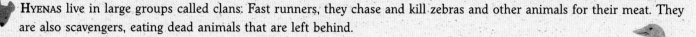

HYENAS live in large groups called clans. Fast runners, they chase and kill zebras and other animals for their meat. They are also scavengers, eating dead animals that are left behind.

OSTRICHES cannot fly. But they can run very fast—up to 40 miles an hour. Ostriches often graze among giraffes and zebras because these hoofed animals alert them when danger is near.

The **AFRICAN ROCK PYTHON** is one of the largest snakes in the world. It is not venomous, but attacks by coiling its bulky body around its prey, constricting it. It swallows its prey whole—even very large animals such as antelopes.

REDBILLED OXPECKERS perch on the bodies of large African mammals. Using their thick red bills, they feed on parasites embedded in the animal's skin. The oxpecker and its host animal are *symbionts*, meaning that both species benefit from living together.

WILDEBEESTS are fast runners that gather in huge herds. They eat mostly grass and are preyed upon by lions and hyenas. Also known as "gnus," their name means "wild beast" in the Afrikaans language. Both males and females have beards, sharp curved horns, and long legs.

RHINOCEROS means "nose horn." All African rhinos have two. If broken off, the horns will grow back. The second largest land mammal after the elephant, rhinos are in danger of extinction because they are often hunted by humans for their horns.

WARTHOGS look fierce but are actually peaceful wild hogs. They generally run and hide rather than fight an enemy. However, warthog mothers fiercely protect their babies. When entering a den, the babies enter first, followed by the mother who enters backwards to protect her piglets with her sharp tusks.

NAKED MOLE RATS are nearly hairless rodents. In some ways they are more like insects, led by a queen rat that breeds the babies and is tended to by the other rats. They spend most of their lives in huge colonies underground, feeding on tubers produced by plants.

SCORPIONS are related to spiders and are arachnids, not insects. They live in underground holes or under rocks during the day and hunt at night. They inject their prey with venom which paralyzes it. Scorpions have been on Earth for millions of years, even before dinosaurs.

LEOPARD TORTOISES are reptiles with attractive markings on their *carapace*—the hard shell which protects their bodies. They retract their head and feet into their shell for protection and sometimes live in abandoned jackal dens. They have been known to live up to 100 years.

About the Animals

ZEBRAS are fast-running mammals that **gallop** on the African savanna to escape from predators like lions and hyenas. They are closely related to horses, with hoofed feet and a long mane. Their hair is white with black stripes. Each zebra has its own unique pattern of stripes, just as humans have unique patterns of fingerprints. Zebras are *herbivores* that spend much of their time grazing. They usually stay together in herds.

GIRAFFES are browsers that **slurp** leaves and twigs with their long, prehensile tongues. Giraffes are the tallest land animal on Earth, from 16 to 19 feet tall. Their legs alone are as tall as a full-grown man, about 6 feet. These *herbivores* prefer to eat from the tops of trees, especially acacia (uh-KAY-shuh) trees, rather than bending down to eat low grasses on the savanna. A giraffe has slimy spit that some people think may coat prickly acacia thorns that could poke its stomach. A baby giraffe is never left alone. If its mother needs to leave to look for food, another mother will look after the baby along with her own.

ELEPHANTS suck water into their trunks and then **squirt** it into their mouths. Some people think they drink water directly through their trunks, but an elephant's trunk is actually an extension of its nose. It is how they breathe. Elephants are very good swimmers. Their huge bodies float and their trunks act like a snorkel. African elephants have few natural enemies; their main enemy is humans. For hundreds of years they have been killed for their ivory tusks, which both males and females have. Elephants are *herbivores*.

HIPPOPOTAMUSES, like most *herbivores*, spend a lot of time **grazing**. Their enormous mouths can open four feet wide. Hippos eat at night and spend a lot of time in water during the day to cool off. Sometimes they may stay completely under water. Hippos are the closest living relatives of whales, and, like whales, females give birth to their calves in the water. Despite its stocky shape, the hippopotamus is a fast runner. It is the third-heaviest land mammal after the elephant and white rhinoceros, weighing up to 4,000 pounds.

LIONS are the largest cats on the African continent. The biggest difference between lions and other cats is that lions are sociable animals that live together in permanent groups called "prides." They are *carnivores*, and the female, the lioness, does most of the hunting. Often hunting in groups, they **stalk** their prey in the long grasses and share the kill with the pride.

CHIMPANZEES are apes, not monkeys. Although most chimps live in tropical rainforests in Africa, they have adapted to other African habitats, including the savanna. Chimps **swing** from trees with their long arms. They are *omnivores* that forage for food during the day. A female chimp usually has her first child around age 14, and infants are dependent upon their mother for about five years. Chimpanzees are an endangered species.

HORNBILLS are *omnivores* that eat mostly fruit, but also insects, snails, crabs, frogs and lizards. Their trumpeting calls vary from a cackle to a **toot**, as they fly around in a 40-foot candelabra tree where the top branches look like cactuses. While the female incubates her eggs, she seals herself into a nest, leaving a small opening so that the male hornbill can bring her food.

AARDVARK are solitary, burrowing mammals. They're *insectivores*, eating only ants and termites. They sometimes travel several miles each night to find large termite mounds. They use their sharp claws to **dig** into the mounds, and then use their pointed snouts and long tongues with sticky saliva to catch the insects. They can close their nostrils to keep dust and insects from invading their snouts. Aardvark look somewhat like pigs, and the name means "earth pig" in the Afrikaans language.

MEERKATS are small mammals about the size of a squirrel with long slender bodies. Their eyes always have black patches around them. They use their long tails as a "third leg" for balance when standing upright. Meerkats live in a group called a "mob" or "gang." They dig burrows to live in with their sharp claws. One meerkat usually stands on guard and **watches** for predators. It warns the group with squeals or barks. They're primarily *insectivores* and are immune to the strong venom of scorpions.

JACKALS are members of the dog family. Both parents take care of their pups, which stay with them until they can establish their own territories. Jackals mark their territory with their urine and feces, and defend their territory from rivals. They **yip and yap** with a wide variety of vocal sounds specific to each jackal family. These *carnivores* hunt mostly at night. Jackals inhabit rocky crevices and dens made by other animals where they sleep during the day to keep cool.

Tips from the Author

This book offers some wonderful opportunities for extended activities and discussions. Here are some suggestions.

Have Fun with Words

🔈 Ten different verbs were used in the story to show how each animal behaves. Act them out as you read or sing the story. I often use puppets to help tell the story. Younger children may want to use masks. See: http://www.enchantedlearning.com/crafts/Masklion.shtml

🔈 Ten different adjectives were used to describe each animal. What are they?

🔈 Make a list of the baby names. Is there one animal that doesn't have a baby name? Research baby names for the hidden animals in the book.

🔈 Introduce new vocabulary. How many animals in the story are *herbivores*? Why are there so many? Who are the *carnivores*? Are there any *omnivores*? What is an *insectivore*?

Who Am I? Write two sentences describing an animal in this book without identifying the animal. Have kids guess the animal, e.g., *I am the tallest mammal on earth. I eat from the tops of trees.*

Counting Fun! Did you notice the African gourd rattles at the bottom of each page? Have children count them from one to ten. Then have them make their own gourd rattles as they sing "Over in the Grasslands." The music is in the back of this book.

Music and Art Music is important in the life of African people, and many instruments are hand-made from nature using wood, gourds, animal horns or skin. To make and decorate a gourd rattle go to: http://www.artistshelpingchildren.org and search for "gourd."

Lion Handprint Painting Have children press one hand (palm and fingers) in orange poster paint. On light green construction paper, instruct them to print a circle of handprints with their palms forming the center of circle. While the paint is drying, give them yellow paper circles to draw eyes, whiskers, and a mouth. Paste the finished yellow circle in the middle of the lion's mane.

Sounds on the Savanna Pretend you are on a safari listening to the sounds you might hear. Use words like *roar, trumpet, bray, toot, yip, scratch, whine, stomp,* and *thunder.* Ask children to name the animal or animals on the African savanna that might make that sound. Have the class make the sound all together. For more ideas about "going on a safari" go to "Activities" at www.dawnpub.com.

Goin' to the Zoo Spend a day with family and friends observing African zoo animals. Take photos and make prints of any animals you see that are in this book. Have your child bring them to his/her class. Students can draw a picture of their favorite photo.

Discover more in books . . .

Starry Safari by Linda Ashman, Harcourt Children's Books

We All Went on a Safari by Laurie Krebs, Barefoot Books

African Critters by Robert Haas, National Geographic Children's Books

Bringing the Rain to Kapiti Plain by Verna Aardema, Puffin Books

Safari, So Good! All About African Animals by Bonnie Worth, Random House

. . . and on the internet

http://www.blueplanetbiomes.org/african_savanna.htm
http://education.nationalgeographic.org/media/
        african-savanna-illustration/
http://kids.nceas.ucsb.edu/biomes/savanna.html
https://nationalzoo.si.edu/Animals/PhotoGallery/AfricanSavanna/

For more curriculum-connection activities, go to www.dawnpub.com and click on "Activities." Scroll to the cover of this book. You will find lesson plans aligned with Common Core and Next Generation Science Standards, along with reproducible bookmarks of the ten main animals in this book and other resources.

Tips from the Illustrator

Animals in their natural habitat can either show up against their background or be able to hide in it. Brightly colored birds that are easy to spot use their pretty feathers to attract their mates. Nature provides other animals with the ability to blend in with their background so they stay camouflaged.

When I was working on the art for this book, a friend was on an African safari. She sent back some wonderful photos. One of the pictures was of a young lion hidden among the tall grasses. The photo was so appealing. I loved the look on the little lion's face and the delicate grasses that the cub was hiding among.

The photo became my inspiration for the lion art. My illustrations are cut paper collages. I make the animals first. Then I look at them on different backgrounds before I decide what I like best. As I cut the pieces, my desk and the area around it become a flurry of bits of colored papers. I use colored pencils and pastels to add detail. The tall grass around the lions is done with colored pencils after all the pieces are glued together. I wanted to show how the animals were camouflaged among the grass, but I also wanted to make sure they showed up. My goal was to keep the beauty of the photo while adding my own artistic ideas.

There are lots of ways we find ideas all around us. As you go through the day, look around and think of what you see that might spark an idea to create something.

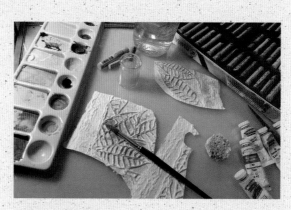

Finding paper for the aardvarks was a challenge.

I crumpled grey paper and used pink pastel.

I chose orange paper for the dirt.

© 2015 Dianne L. Ochiltree.

Over in the Grasslands

Sung to the tune "Over in the Meadow"

Traditional Tune
Words by Marianne Berkes

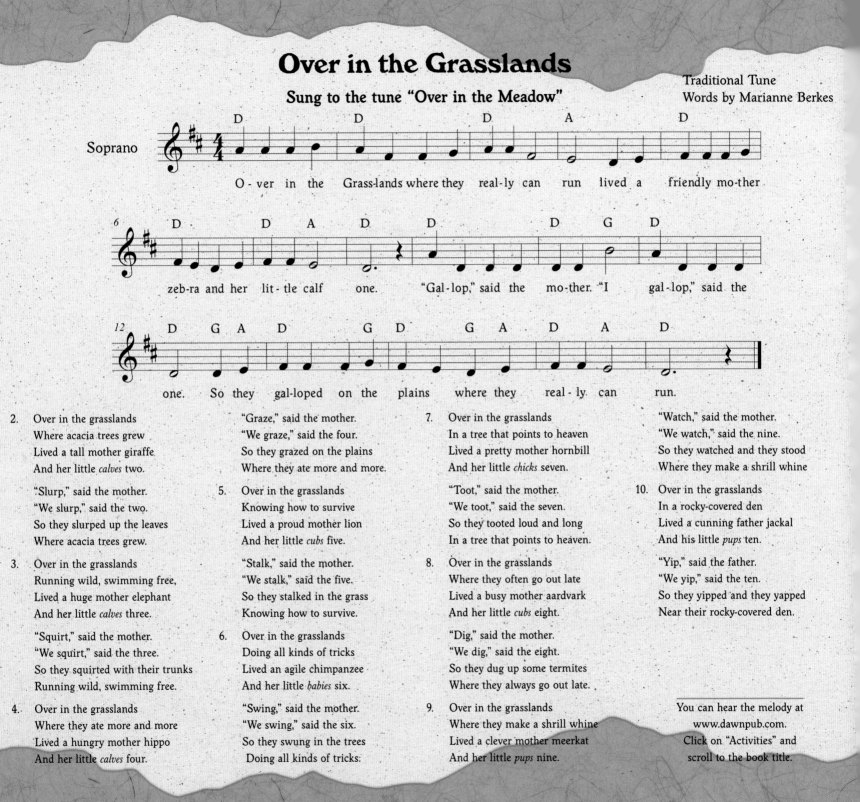

Soprano

O-ver in the Grass-lands where they real-ly can run lived a friendly mo-ther

zeb-ra and her lit-tle calf one. "Gal-lop," said the mo-ther. "I gal-lop," said the

one. So they gal-loped on the plains where they real-ly can run.

2. Over in the grasslands
Where acacia trees grew
Lived a tall mother giraffe
And her little *calves* two.

"Slurp," said the mother.
"We slurp," said the two.
So they slurped up the leaves
Where acacia trees grew.

3. Over in the grasslands
Running wild, swimming free,
Lived a huge mother elephant
And her little *calves* three.

"Squirt," said the mother.
"We squirt," said the three.
So they squirted with their trunks
Running wild, swimming free.

4. Over in the grasslands
Where they ate more and more
Lived a hungry mother hippo
And her little *calves* four.

"Graze," said the mother.
"We graze," said the four.
So they grazed on the plains
Where they ate more and more.

5. Over in the grasslands
Knowing how to survive
Lived a proud mother lion
And her little *cubs* five.

"Stalk," said the mother.
"We stalk," said the five.
So they stalked in the grass
Knowing how to survive.

6. Over in the grasslands
Doing all kinds of tricks
Lived an agile chimpanzee
And her little *babies* six.

"Swing," said the mother.
"We swing," said the six.
So they swung in the trees
Doing all kinds of tricks:

7. Over in the grasslands
In a tree that points to heaven
Lived a pretty mother hornbill
And her little *chicks* seven.

"Toot," said the mother.
"We toot," said the seven.
So they tooted loud and long
In a tree that points to heaven.

8. Over in the grasslands
Where they often go out late
Lived a busy mother aardvark
And her little *cubs* eight.

"Dig," said the mother.
"We dig," said the eight.
So they dug up some termites
Where they always go out late.

9. Over in the grasslands
Where they make a shrill whine
Lived a clever mother meerkat
And her little *pups* nine.

"Watch," said the mother.
"We watch," said the nine.
So they watched and they stood
Where they make a shrill whine

10. Over in the grasslands
In a rocky-covered den
Lived a cunning father jackal
And his little *pups* ten.

"Yip," said the father.
"We yip," said the ten.
So they yipped and they yapped
Near their rocky-covered den.

You can hear the melody at
www.dawnpub.com.
Click on "Activities" and
scroll to the book title.

MARIANNE BERKES has spent much of her life as a teacher, children's theater director and children's librarian and puts these experiences to good use in over 20 entertaining and educational picture books that make a child's learning relevant. Reading, music and theater have been a constant in Marianne's life. Her books are also inspired by her love of nature. She hopes to open kids' eyes to the magic found in our natural world. Marianne now writes full time. She is an energetic presenter at schools and literary conferences nationwide. Her website is www.MarianneBerkes.com.

JILL DUBIN's whimsical art has appeared in over 30 children's books. Her cut paper illustrations reflect her interest in combining color, pattern and texture. She grew up in Yonkers, New York, and graduated from Pratt Institute. She lives with her family in Atlanta, Georgia, including two dogs that do very little but with great enthusiasm. www.JillDubin.com

DEDICATIONS

For Jill Dubin, whose spectacular illustrations make my words come alive. How grateful I am for her richly-textured cut paper art in the six "Over" books we have done together. — MB

To Cecilia Belle with love. — JD

Book design and computer production by
Patty Arnold, *Menagerie Design & Publishing*

DAWN PUBLICATIONS

12402 Bitney Springs Road
Nevada City, CA 95959
530-274-7775
nature@dawnpub.com

Library of Congress Cataloging-in-Publication Data
Names: Berkes, Marianne Collins. | Dubin, Jill, illustrator.
Title: Over in the grasslands : on an African savanna / by Marianne Berkes ; illustrated by Jill Dubin.
Description: First edition. | Nevada City, CA : Dawn Publications, [2016] |
   Summary: This grasslands variation of the classic song "Over in the Meadow" introduces animals and their offspring that dwell on the savanna of Africa, from a mother zebra and her "little calf one" to a "cunning father jackal and his little pups ten." Includes information about the African savanna, a glossary of the animals, activities, and other "tips from the author." | Includes bibliographical references.
Identifiers: LCCN 2016000358 | ISBN 9781584695677 (hardback) | ISBN 9781584695684 (pbk.)
Subjects: | CYAC: Stories in rhyme. | Grassland animals–Fiction. Animals–Africa–Fiction. | Counting.
Classification: LCC PZ8.3.B4557 Ow 2016 | DDC [E]–dc23 LC record available at http://lccn.loc.gov/2016000358

Manufactured by Regent Publishing Services, Hong Kong
Printed May, 2016, in ShenZhen, Guangdong, China

10 9 8 7 6 5 4 3 2 1
First Edition

Also by Marianne Berkes

Over in the Ocean: In a Coral Reef — With unique and outstanding style, this book portrays a vivid community of marine creatures.

Over in the Jungle: A Rainforest Rhyme — As with *Ocean*, this book captures a rain forest teeming with remarkable animals.

Over in the Forest: Come and Take a Peek — Follow the tracks of forest animals, but watch out for the skunk!

Over in the Arctic: Where the Cold Winds Blow — Another charming counting rhyme introduces creatures of the tundra.

Over in Australia: Amazing Animals Down Under — Australian animals are often unique, many with pouches for the babies. Such fun!

Over in a River: Flowing Out to the Sea — Beavers, manatees and so many more animals help teach the geography of 10 great North American rivers.

Over on a Mountain: Somewhere in the World — Twenty cool animals, ten great mountain ranges, and seven continents all in one story!

Over on the Farm — Welcome to the farm, where pigs roll, goats nibble, horses gallop, hens peck, and turkeys strut! Count, clap, and sing along.

Going Around the Sun: Some Planetary Fun — Earth is part of a fascinating "family" of planets. Here's a glimpse of the "neighborhood."

Seashells by the Seashore — Kids discover, identify, and count twelve beautiful shells to give Grandma for her birthday.

Going Home: The Mystery of Animal Migration — Many animals migrate "home," often over great distances. A solid introduction to the phenomenon of migration.

The Swamp Where Gator Hides — Still as a log, only his watchful eyes can be seen. But when gator moves, he really moves!

What's in the Garden? — Good food doesn't begin on a store shelf in a box. It comes from a garden bursting with life!

Baby on Board: How Animal Parents Carry Their Young – coming in 2017

A Few Other Nature Awareness Books from Dawn Publications

The Prairie That Nature Built — A romp above, below, and all around a beautiful and exciting habitat. There's nothing boring about a prairie!

Mighty Mole and Super Soil — Below your feet, Mighty Mole is on the move, like a swimmer in dirt. Her largely invisible ecosystem is vital to the health of the world.

Pitter and Patter — Take a ride a water cycle with Pitter and Patter, two drops of water! You'll go through a watershed, down, around, and up again. Oh, the places you'll go . . .

The Mouse in the Meadow — A curious young mouse boldly ventures into the meadow. There he gets a crash course about life from creatures both friendly and not so friendly.

On Kiki's Reef — Swim with Kiki, a baby sea turtle, as she grows to become a gentle giant ad discovers life n a busy coral reef with lots of surprises!

Noisy Bug Sing-Along — There's a lot going on out there in the remarkable, noisy world of insects — and they're all very closeup! Also sing-along with *Noisy Frog* and *Noisy Bird*.

Dandelion Seed's Big Dream — A charming tale that follows a seed as it floats from the countryside to the city and encounters all sorts of obstacles and opportunities.

A Moon of My Own — An adventurous young girl journeys around the world accompanied by her faithful companion, the Moon. Wonder and beauty await you.

Dawn Publications is dedicated to inspiring in children a deeper understanding and appreciation for all life on Earth. You can browse through our titles, download resources for teachers, and order at www.dawnpub.com, or call 800-545-7475.